THE COWARD OF GRIMSBY

ERIC DANIEL RYAN

MAPLE STREET BOOKS

ISBN 978-1-7378144-1-2 paperback

ISBN 978-1-7378144-0-5 ebook

Cover design by nskvsky

For my treasures
Cory, Casey, and Sawyer Bean

THE COWARD OF GRIMSBY

I n the complicated case of Cornelius Braddock, history must look to the long tradition of English maritime law to sort out the multiple facets of the predicament. The case brought before the tribunal in 1897 bewildered all who heard the tale. It concerned the widower Braddock, thought to be lost at sea only to wash up on the shores of France with a grim story of mutiny and long-lost treasure.

The day following news of Braddock's reappearance, *The London Tribune,* as well as *The Tattler* and *The Morning Zephyr*, ran rampant with speculation about his miraculous return. Once the articles circulated, he was labeled a coward and a cutthroat. The consensus among the dockworkers along the harbor, from the wharfinger to the stevedores, was that his story reeked of deceit, and the long months lost at sea gave him ample time to concoct a story that placed blame on his missing crew. The only man who lent any credence to his claims was Georges Dufort, a one-legged French fisherman turned transient, who was himself looked down upon with a healthy degree of skepticism.

Georges Dufort's arrival in the port city of Grimsby, England in search of a partner and bene-factor was the catalyst of the tragic turn of events. After years of postponement, he discovered new information regarding an old family legend and finally embarked on the adventure that played out many times in his dreams. Now an older man with a walrus–tusk beard hiding most of his wrinkles and with nothing left to lose, he booked passage from France across the English Channel.

After Georges' arrival on the steamship *Sussex* at the Royal Docks in Grimsby, he set out in search of a ship and a captain. Not fluent in the Queen's English, he clutched his tattered pea coat close and wandered about the company slips, gutting stalls, and countless fishing trawlers, waving a rolled parchment in the air, calling out in his native tongue to any who would listen.

"*This is a map to untold riches. Who among you wishes to share in its glory?*"

Georges recited his plea desperately to no avail. He cursed everyone around him for not bothering to learn the language of their neighbors. Eventually, the smell of spirits on his breath grew stronger.

He spent twenty-nine days canvasing the Royal pier and the fish docks, trying to recruit a crew for his adventure. He promised an abundance of riches to any man who was seaworthy and willing to lead the expedition. He quickly became a regular, sprawled out in coils of rope or fishing nets, sleeping off his drunkenness. He subsisted on discarded ale and pilfered fish heads from the fishmongers' stalls. He was spat upon and shunned—looked down upon as the scourge of society.

On the thirtieth day in the unforgiving port city,

a well-known aristocrat named Cornelius Braddock answered his prayers. As Georges shuffled about on his familiar path, Braddock stood with the toes of his boots over the pier's edge, staring quietly off into the ocean with a gentle sway to his body. While most heard the desperation in the beggar's plea, Braddock heard something that uncovered memories buried deep below his sadness; the French accent of his long-deceased mother. Her smile flashed brightly in the darkness. He wished she could hold him now. The scent of her delectable vichyssoise floated on the sound, landing gently on his palette. He tasted leek and marjoram on his tongue.

"This is a map to untold riches. Who among you wishes to share in its glory?"

Braddock offered the man as much smile as he could muster and addressed him in astonishingly adept French, matching the regional dialect.

"Pardon me, sir, may I be of help to you?"

Georges' eyes welled. His chin quivered.

"Yes. Please, sir. I have been trying to get someone's attention for weeks. I am so hungry. If you help me with a meal and regaining my wits, I have a wonderful story to tell you and perhaps an opportunity to repay your kindness."

In recent days Braddock was tormented by a calling to walk headlong into the sea and disappear under the white caps. Memories of his beloved Rebecca weighed heavily on his wilting frame. Only five days ago, the gravediggers lowered her corpse into the mass grave with the rest of the dead. He watched from afar as they set fire to everything he ever loved, leaving him to wander the world alone.

The least he could offer the man who spoke in his mother's tongue was a meal and a friendly ear if only to stem the visions. Braddock led the man to a nearby oyster stall, where they swatted away the gulls and helped themselves to seats on the wooden stools near the edge of the pier.

Georges' eyes grew threefold when the surly gentleman who tended the oyster stall appeared with two large pewter mugs, ale spilling over the rims.

"Would you like some oysters, or eel pie, perhaps?" Braddock asked.

Georges gulped down the ale in a single up-ending of his mug. After returning it to the table, he wiped the remnants away from his dreadful beard and nodded vigorously.

"Please."

After a dozen channel oysters, an assortment of other provisions from the sea, two more beverages, and a deep belch from within, Georges' hunger subsided, and he was ready to tell Braddock his tale of riches and adventure. As the story escaped through Georges' twisted mustache and knotted whiskers, Braddock found himself slowly drifting forward on his stool, hanging on the words, the spark of something flourishing.

IN 1808, after the culmination of the French Revolutionary Wars and the coronation of young King Ferdinand VII of Spain, a rumor began to spread across the border that Ferdinand's short reign was in jeopardy. With the devastating armies of the French Emperor Napoleon Bonaparte on the march, the court of the newly crowned Spanish monarch advised him to dispatch a ship to abscond with the country's gold reserves so the riches wouldn't fall into the hands of the enemy. This clandestine ship, loaded down with 32-pounder cannons and a skeleton crew, was underway shortly afterward. It followed a course that took it south to the remote island of Annobón, far off Africa's western coast. Here its coffers were to be hidden away with a small group of colonists loyal to the Spanish crown. They were to keep the king's wealth untouched during the tumult that lay ahead.

But the ship never reached port in Annobón.

Before any word of the voyage's outcome reached the young King Ferdinand, he was forced to abdicate his throne to Emperor Napoleon. After word of this ship reached Napoleon, he questioned Ferdinand on the matter. Ferdinand denied he ever dispatched a vessel and that mobs plundered his gold before his abdication. He claimed that the ship was a rumor, and his wealth was scattered throughout the countryside. Growing tired of the charade and unimpressed by his deceit, Napoleon placed Ferdinand under heavy guard at the Chateau de Valencay in France. Ferdinand dutifully held his tongue throughout his years of captivity, but no word of the treasure ever reached him. Napoleon and his earnest military mind eventually thought better of wasting his assets searching for the treasure and aimed his attention toward other worthwhile adversaries and more considerable conquests. Neither the fabled treasure nor the galleon that carried it was ever seen or heard from again.

~

GEORGES CRADLED the rolled parchment in his palms like an offering to the gods of persuasion.

"This, my new friend, is a message meant for King Ferdinand from the only surviving member of the doomed voyage. The ship went down in a storm just shy of reaching its destination. After the ship-wreck, this lone survivor was adrift off the eastern shores of Annobón when he was eventually rescued by a passing French expedition on its return from the southern shores of Africa. Sadly, this expedition encountered the British royal navy off the coast of France and was captured by the HMS *Victorious*. The crew was taken prisoner, but this lone survivor was able to escape before the prison ships sailed for England and found refuge in the north of France where he lived out the rest of his days, in secret."

Braddock held up a hand between them as Georges' excitement was getting the best of him. Georges settled back on his stool and took a breath.

"This is a truly remarkable story, Georges, but it feels like just that, a story. A legend said to children before bedtime."

"Mr. Braddock, this is the proof that the story is true," Georges said, still holding up the parchment. He forced it into Braddock's hands.

"And how did you come to possess this message?" Braddock asked.

"The story and this message were passed on to me by the lone survivor of the king's voyage. My grandfather."

"Your grandfather?"

Georges nodded slowly.

Braddock read the weathered parchment with wide eyes. He ran his fingertip over the stiff, saffron–hued paper as his lips moved along with the words.

His eyes traced the remnants of the Spanish royal coat of arms stamped in red wax at the top center. He recognized the design, but this one had the addition of what appeared to be a large crown resting at the top. Underneath the seal was a now–faded message written in elegant calligraphy. Braddock could discern the heart of the message from the sparse Spanish he could understand: words like *mission, invasion, island, gold, Annobón, safekeeping, dispatch, war*. At the bottom was something he didn't need any knowledge of the Spanish language to understand. It was an unmistakable and ostentatious signature.

Ferdinand Vii, Rey de España.

He turned the parchment over and studied the back closely. There was no writing but what appeared to be a rudimentary sketch of the western coast of Africa and a tiny island chain. Just to the east of the southernmost island was a small black *X*. Next to it was one word.

Aquí.

Here.

"Why did your grandfather not report this to the king after the war?"

"After the king was reinstated to the throne, he became known as *El Rey Felón*. The Felon King. The country was impoverished and split under his rule. My grandfather was no longer loyal to the crown. By that time, he had met my grandmother and fallen madly in love. He told me he refused to risk his life once again for another man's treasure. He said he already had all the treasure he could ever want."

Braddock felt the well inside himself rising to the surface. He felt the levees about to break.

"You are telling me the truth?" Braddock asked.

Georges nodded again before taking a long sip of his ale.

With his hand over his mouth, Braddock read the letter another time before standing from his stool and turning a slow half-circle to face the ocean. He stared out at the choppy surface and gazed upon the white caps splashing saltwater spray upon the pier.

"Annobón?" said Braddock.

"Yes sir."

"How many fathoms down is the ship?" Braddock asked.

"I am not sure, perhaps ten or twelve, but we will require a diving bell and someone experienced with its operation."

Nothing remained here for Braddock except death and reminders of his sweet Rebecca. Perhaps it was preferable to sail away on the open ocean instead of stepping headlong into it. Maybe this mysterious fisherman was an angel washed ashore, ready to guide him to salvation.

He spoke with his back to Georges, addressing the sea.

"This treasure, it is worth your life?"

Georges raised himself straight with a minor wobble in his movement—the fault of the ale, no doubt—and joined Braddock at the pier's edge. They shared a glance and a quarter smile of agreement, and Georges knew that he had found himself a captain.

"Have you been on many voyages before?" Georges asked.

"These are times for new adventures, my friend. We shall leave the old ones ashore."

"Where did you learn your French, sir?" Georges asked.

"My mother was born in Saint-Malo, in Brittany, and spoke only French to me until her death when I was a young man."

"Well then, we are practically countrymen. Now let us stop wasting time and find a worthy ship," said Georges.

"Leave that to me. I will get us a ship and a crew by the week's end."

Braddock raised his empty mug to the keeper of the oyster stall, signaling his need for a further drink. "Two of your finest, good sir. We must celebrate our new partnership."

The barman obliged, retrieving two fresh mugs filled to the rim.

"To adventure," said Georges, raising his glass.

"To Ferdinand," said Braddock, tapping his mug to the rim of his partner's.

"To Napoleon."

"And the high seas."

They drank until the cups ran dry.

AFTER A WEEK OF INQUIRIES, Braddock woke with a sense of purpose that he hadn't felt in some time. A sense of purpose *and* a ravishing hangover. After spending the week canvassing the port city's underbelly and imbibing heavily into the early morning hours, they were finally successful in their ventures, having secured the necessary provisions for their voyage.

Braddock looked around his lavish home in the

much-desired east side of Grimsby and was still pleased with the gentlemen's agreement he had entered. He assured Georges that he would deliver a vessel by week's end, and he had most certainly followed through on his promise. The tavern they chose to patronize was not by chance. It was known to be frequented not only by local whalers and fishermen but by cavalier aristocrats of lesser scruples searching for things that were not allowed on the surface of refined English society. After finding a mark, Braddock offered his home, possessions, and equal share of the treasure to a low-level officer of the *Grimsby Deep Sea Fishing Company* whose ambition for advancement knew no bounds. Once the man learned the extent of Braddock's holdings, he was enthusiastic in offering the seasoned captain and weathered crew of a sixty-foot trawler, along with the use of the ship itself. It was once a fishing vessel but was newly refurbished for salvage and dock work. It certainly helped that Braddock's holdings were worth double that of the cost of the ship. It also didn't hurt that the company man possessed questionable morals, gambling debts, and a high percentage of ale in his bloodstream.

There was no hesitation on Braddock's part once he made up his mind. Quietly wandering around his home that morning, he was reminded too often of his sweet Rebecca. He averted his gaze from the collection of deathly souvenirs that filled every corner of every room. He recognized her shape embedded in the chaise lounge fabric under the street-side windows, where she would read and bathe in sunlight in the late summer afternoons. A few of her favorite Dutch chocolates melted streams of dark sugar down the pillows and onto the floor. The last dishes she ate from remained unwashed on her nightstand, inviting flies and growing mold in the summer heat. The roll of green silk that lay unspooled on their drawing room floor would never take another form or have new life. Nothing remained for him here. All the trappings of their wealth were no longer of need to him, and the memories they held would only weigh him down in the water.

It was time.

He gathered a few personal belongings and put them in his leather satchel: a pen and journal, a gold timepiece, a daguerreotype photograph of his late wife, and the small French-made compass she gave him on his last birthday. He didn't look back as he closed the door to his former home and marched toward the docks where his adventure was to begin.

After searching the slips of the Grimsby shipyard, he finally laid his eyes upon the salvage vessel and the eight men hired to accompany him on this expedition. He approached a herculean man at the bottom of the gangway and stood in his shadow.

"Mr. Gibson, I presume? It is a pleasure to meet you," Braddock said, holding out his hand.

The previous captain of his newly acquired ship, the burly seafarer, Solomon Gibson, did not return the offered greeting. Braddock, dressed more for a foxhunt than a long voyage on the open ocean, did not seem to impress the seasoned veteran of the high seas. Solomon spat a cheek-full of tobacco juice onto the dock, a string of it hanging on his lower lip.

"We shove off with the tide, rich man," Solomon said.

"Very well, sir. I look forward to this journey

with you," Braddock replied, feeling the chill in the air. "Can I be of any assistance?"

He leaned down to pick up a loaded burlap sack, and Solomon snatched it from him, looking him up and down.

"All you need to hold up is your end of the bargain, rich man. Double wages when we return from this idiotic venture of yours."

"Of course, sir," Braddock replied.

He could feel the eyes of the bedraggled crew upon him as he cautiously backed away from Solomon and set out for the final time to reconvene with Georges and embark on their journey.

He entered the White Horse Tavern and Inn and went directly to the room he had rented for Georges, but only silence greeted him. He expected a one-legged Frenchmen snoring the ale away but found a bed that was unslept in.

"Have you seen my friend? The Frenchman with the large walrus–tusk beard?" he asked the old innkeeper.

"He never returned last night, sir," she replied through bear trap teeth.

Braddock searched that evening but to no avail. After reluctantly telling Solomon that their departure would be delayed and agreeing to pay the crew for another day's work, he continued searching. When the following evening approached and he had not found Georges, he came to terms with the fact that he would be venturing alone on this quest. Without the man who made all this possible. He remained firm in his intention to give Georges a fair share of the treasure once it was in hand. Braddock returned to the White Horse Tavern and paid Georges' room for three months of lodging, hoping he would make his return. On the way out, he gave a parcel to the owner of the Inn, instructing her to keep it until Georges returned, which he prayed would be soon.

With loose ends tied up and the evening tides receding, he boarded the ship. Thoughts of an African sunset stirred the virgin explorer in Braddock and began to wash away his misery. He made his way to the deck of the ship with the rolled parchment in one hand and his coat clutched in the other. With a breeze running east to west, he stood on the leeward side of the ship and watched the gathering of masts and sails fade away, wishing Georges Dufort the best in life.

SEVEN MONTHS LATER, a stout boy named Pierre—who the court stenographer recorded as *Peere* in the Magistrate's notes—walked the shores of Brittany, France. He used the heel of his boot to construct a series of canals in the sand alongside the saltwater pools created when the tide recedes. On the quiet end of the previous night's storm, as he always does, he scoured the beach for some ocean debris and hopefully a handful of bouchot mussels that the violence of the waves had freed.

After filling his basket with a few tiny treasures, he happened upon a small, damaged vessel capsized at the waterline. Peering over the upturned hull, he discovered a man's lifeless body, stark naked and tangled in the rigging. Pierre grasped a nearby length of beach wood and, brushing the dark curly hair from his eyes, prodded the sunburnt corpse. On the third jab, the body coughed up a lungful of saltwater. Pierre squealed and fled home, where he knew his mother would be in the kitchen at that very moment, baking her heavenly pain au chocolat.

He exploded through the door into their modest kitchen and straight into the fragrant smell coming from the oven. He nearly forgot what his commotion was about when the scent of warm chocolate and fresh pastry wafted up in his nostrils, but his mother's shrieking reminded him.

"For heaven's sake, Pierre. What on Earth has gotten into you?"

"There is a man. Down near the water's edge," he said breathlessly. "His boat has washed ashore. I thought he was dead. And his manhood is out."

"What did your father tell you about saying such things, Pierre?"

"No, Mother, it's true. There is a real boat with a real man. I know it. I poked him with a stick."

"You know your father is too sick to deal with more of this non-sense, my love. And I must finish these pastries for Madame Cuvier, or I will not be paid."

Pierre stood motionless, his eyes imploring her to believe him.

After a moment, his mother smiled, untied the flour-covered apron from her waist, and hung it neatly on a small hook tucked just behind the open door, causing the loose flour to fall to the wooden floorboards in a small cloud.

Pierre led her down a stone path through an opening in the ramparts, connecting their family's small seaside home with the shore. As they walked over the crest of a bluff, she saw the man, laying prone in the sand and bound to the broken mast, completely tangled in the rigging. Neither clothing nor sail preserving his modesty. Just a heap of rope wrapped precariously around his skeletal frame.

She approached him cautiously, averting her eyes from what lay exposed for all of God and country to see.

"Monsieur? Monsieur? Can you hear me?"

She crept to within arms-length of the body, planning to jostle him slightly, when he spontaneously burst into a coughing fit.

"Pierre, help me get him to the house."

Pierre did not hear her. He was standing quite a distance back from the scene, ravenously eating a warm pain au chocolat, stolen while his mother's back was turned and wearing the dark evidence of the crime on his face.

Cornelius Braddock awoke the following morning to the gentle hand of Murielle Fournier, Pierre's mother, tending to his fever. A slow drip of water cascaded down his face from a cool, wet cloth dabbed at his forehead. Before that moment, his last recollection was of a mighty wind and a great wave pushing his small sail into the sea. While adjusting to the morning light, he smelled the sweet and savory scent of freshly baked bread and crispy bacon and, for a moment, believed he was dead and had awoken in Heaven. He thought this, all the while staring up at the angelic features of Murielle's face as she spooned a salty chicken broth into his mouth, reviving his soul. The morning sun cast a halo around her espresso hair.

"Where am I?" he asked the angel.

"Je ne comprends pas, monsieur," she replied softly.

"Where am I?" he asked again in French.

"Saint-Malo, monsieur. In Brittany."

It was the way his mother used to say it.

Murielle tended to his minor wounds and sun blisters, nursing his broken spirit back to health over the following days. He awoke in the mornings to the smell of her confections baking in the kitchen. The scent wafted up the stairs into his room when Pierre opened and closed the back door on his way to search the beach each day for items to fill his collections and possibly their plates. Braddock grew accustomed to the series of footfalls and bangs and clangs and latches closing. He awaited the sugar floating on air to reach him after each succession.

In the afternoons, when the cottage was empty, Braddock and Murielle shared stories from their lives. They sat together near the open windows, feeling the northern breeze pass through the rooms, carrying the lace curtains in spirals on the air.

He talked of his mother from Brittany and the happiness he felt at finally seeing where she was born, and she spoke of her husband's illness and the sorrow she felt with being unable to provide for her family. He told her of his dear Rebecca and her good nature and sweet voice, and she told him of Pierre's boisterous spirit and his burgeoning collections.

She shared stories of how her great grand-mother once baked her family's famous pain au chocolat for Napoleon and his court during a brief reprieve they took in Saint-Malo many years before. It was the same recipe that Murielle became known for baking throughout the province. The very one that earned her family a meager wage and helped nurse Braddock back to health. Braddock told her his tale of Napoleon and King Ferdinand and royal gold, eventually telling her the story of his harrowing and cursed journey.

They passed the time together through these friendly conversations and sunny afternoons. It was the happiest time Braddock could remember.

As the Fourniers aided his return from the dark abscess of starvation and sickness, news of his reappearance eventually circulated back across the channel with the daily imports and exports of local merchants. Reports of him washing ashore reached the upper levels of the English aristocracy, and imaginations ran rampant with speculation about the fate of his voyage.

It wasn't long before the Grimsby Deep Sea Fishing Company sent an emissary to the Fournier family's residence to confirm the shipwrecked man's identity and escort him home to answer for what became of the missing ship and her crew.

Braddock bid farewell to his gracious hosts with his identity confirmed and once again took to the seas, watching Murielle and Pierre fade away as his ship made passage home. The white cliffs of Dover bid him and his chaperones a warm welcome as the noisy ocean gulls ferried them across the channel, mistaking the small transport for a trawler and pestering it for an errant fish. A sobering realization washed over him as they made a final maneuver into the harbor at Grimsby, and he saw the massive crowd awaiting his return. His insides went topsy-turvy, and his heart raced.

Buried deeply within the ravenous crowd that day was a healthy and very much alive Georges Dufort, who was able to catch a brief yet unrecognizable glimpse of his partner as he was escorted off the ship. The slip they occupied on the Royal Docks was mobbed, and the scene that unfolded was one of heartbreak. The families of the men hired by

Braddock crowded around to look at the man dis-
embarking the vessel. Word spread that he was the
only surviving member of the crew, but with fleeting
hope, the families watched still as he was guided
down the gangway and onto the docks, alone.

He was pelted with horse mud and rotten food
as jeers and threats erupted from the crowd.

"Coward!"

"Deserter!"

"Murderer!"

"Jellyfish!"

"Are they all dead?"

"Should the captain not go down with the ship?"

Accusations were hurled at him, followed by the
sobbing of the women, whose last shred of hope was
ripped from them. With nobody following him off
the ship, they were widows again and their children
still fatherless.

Braddock was diverted to the nearest carriage
and whisked from the scene before any harm could
come to him. The port of Grimsby was a fisherman's
haven, ruled mainly through maritime law and the
unwritten customs of men that spend their lives on
the water. It was no longer a safe place for Braddock.

Nearly five weeks passed before Georges bribed
his way into the county jail where Braddock was
being held. He was deeply saddened after discov-
ering that Braddock was remanded to the horren-
dousness of the solitary cells. Where Braddock
recently sailed upon the ocean with space enough to
spread his arms wide in each direction, he now
stood in the darkest of holes, cast down into the
depths of the Earth with the monsters and the
troglodytes. In his cell, he stretched out his arms in
the darkness to the stones just above his head, and

his fingers touched the walls before his elbows fully unbent.

Georges entered the cramped cell neighboring Braddock and stood idle while his eyes adjusted to the darkness. The scribbles of madmen became visible on the moss-covered walls.

Eventually, he could hear Braddock's mutterings in the silence.

"Mr. Braddock? It is your partner, Georges Dufort. I am here."

The murmuring ceased, and Georges practically heard Braddock's mind wondering if the voice was a figment of his solitude.

"I am in the next cell. I came to check on your health and to hear of your journey."

"Georges, is that you?"

"It is sir."

"How did you get here? What happened to you?"

Georges paused and looked at his feet. "I am sorry to say that the night before we were to embark on our treasure hunt, I let the drink get the best of me. In the celebration of my good fortune, I fell and hit my head. A good samaritan took me to a nearby convalescence home, but by the time I awoke, you were already gone."

"I received the parcel you left with the innkeeper. I sold the wedding ring inside according to your instructions, and for that I thank you. It was truly a treasure to behold. The proceeds have supported me these many months, and the last of it I used as payment to allow us these few brief moments together."

Georges heard a slight sniffle through the wall.

"How long have I been here?"

"More than a month, sir."

"And will they release me?"

"I do not think so."

"Georges, please, you must listen to me. They are saying I am a coward and a fraud. That I have invented this story to save myself, but you must believe me. I am as certain as I have ever been about what happened on the African coast."

His voice became frantic, and through the walls, Georges heard feet scuffling quickly along the dirt floor. Georges said nothing.

"Are you there?" Braddock searched for contact as his question lingered without a response.

"I am," replied Georges.

"Do you blame me as well?"

"Well, sir, if I blame you, then I would have to blame myself. I was the one who shared the secret with you, and if not for my untimely accident, I would have shared the same fate as the crew. God rest their souls."

"Our ship didn't go down, Georges. The crew was not lost at sea. If they have not killed each other yet over their share of the treasure, then they live as rich men. In Africa."

"You found the treasure?" asked Georges.

"I did, sir. I swear it on the memory of my dear Rebecca."

Georges' life had reached a tipping point when he discovered the parchment tucked away in the fishing vessel he inherited from his father. He remembered feeling a pivotal moment rush by him. He could either lean whole-heartedly into the incredible tale of the long-lost treasure or tuck the letter away, remanding it deep within the hull of the ship carrying all his forgotten things. He chose to leave all behind and believe. To venture out in his old age and breath in the air of adventure and open ocean. Until now, he wasn't sure if he had ever really believed in the treasure. Braddock's conviction sat in his belly like a colony of butterflies waiting to spread their wings and take flight.

"I haven't much time, my friend. There is talk of the gallows for you. They are searching for answers to the death of the eight sailors and the loss of the ship. The company–man you made a deal with was killed over a gambling debt just days after your departure and can't verify your claims. I needn't tell you of the immense power of the Grimsby Deep Sea Fishing Company, and I am afraid you have crossed them. They wish to make an example of you. Now, I will tell you what I know of your case, but first, tell me what happened. Tell me of the treasure."

FROM THE MOMENT they raised the anchor, the crew neither trusted nor respected Braddock. Solomon, the previous–and true–captain of the ship, was not one to take orders, especially from an aristocrat who displayed no ability to navigate the open seas. He held his tongue and scratched at his wind-chapped face as Braddock's poor skills were on display. After several days of ineptitude, the angered crew treated him with deep disdain, and Solomon could no longer bite his tongue.

While believing his crumb of seafaring knowledge would suffice in sailing all the way past the equator, Braddock was quickly in over his head. A storm swept in on the fourth night of the voyage, and the orders he gave were less than amateur, resulting in the near-death of a crew member. Forced to admit his inexperience to Solomon and the crew, Braddock reluctantly shared the details of the voyage. He told them of George's story, the letter, and the true bounty awaiting them. Unfortunately for Braddock, he was a stranger on a tight-knit ship and underestimated how long years on the open water could bring men together and change their souls.

It would have been a mutiny if Braddock was indeed the ship's captain, but he knew better. He proved to be nothing more than a passenger on an arduous voyage that the real captain and his men were now undertaking. Within a week, he was banished below deck and became subject to near starvation and regular beatings from the increasingly drunken crew. He couldn't tell how much time passed before they finally anchored in the crystal waters off the shores of Annobón, but it felt like a lifetime.

Braddock was finally released from the belly of the ship, and the sun greeted him. He felt the sun's rays reach through his eyes and sear the back of his skull. He required a significant length of time to regain his eyesight, but a vision of paradise took shape when he did.

Before their departure, it was agreed upon that one of the crew would descend into the shipwreck, but they now informed Braddock that he would be plunged deep into the savage green and blue of the ocean. He explained that he had no experience under a diving bell, but it proved a useless protest. Once the diving bell was ready to deploy, Braddock found himself entombed in the bell-shaped metal contraption, sinking towards the bottom of the ocean and the treasure of all lifetimes.

The pocket of air created as the bell dropped to

the bottom of the ocean was a terrifying place to be. With only enough room for his head to remain above water, he felt as though he would never see the surface again. Looking down past his floating legs at the clear blue beneath him, he watched the ocean floor materialize. The inhabitants of the underwater world paid no attention to the intruder and his otherworldly ship. It was only moments before he saw the unmistakable outline of the Spanish warship beneath him.

The clarity of the ocean was astounding. With his bare feet now in the sand and his lungs full of oxygen, Braddock dunked his head into the salty water and swam out from under the diving bell. A pressure unlike any he felt before exploded in his ears, nearly knocking the wind out of him. His eyes adjusted to the salinity of the water.

From the seabed, the outline he saw on his descent was a colossal heap of timbers, a ship reclaimed by the Earth. Schools of strange-looking fish swam through the portholes, and tattered remnants of canvas sail floated gently in the current, pinned down by the weight of barnacle-covered cannons. On his first few attempts to leave the safety of the diving bell, his body shook uncontrollably from fear but, as he ventured out farther and farther from the bell, he collected strength and composure in the deep.

After a dozen more descents, Braddock discovered an opening in the bilge which led to the coffers within. He brushed away hundreds of pink and grey African ghost crabs from the wooden chests with his hands. As they scattered in all directions, a likeness of the Spanish royal coat of arms revealed itself to be branded in the wood. He recognized the charred circle with a crowned lion and castle from its image scrawled on the parchment.

After countless trips down in the diving bell, he secured the bounty, and the crew above raised it from its resting place. Once the last chest was excavated from the deep, Braddock resurfaced for the last time and stood back from them on the ship's deck. He stood with eyes wide and shivered from countless days of descending and ascending in the cold of the ocean. He dreamt this moment would be a glorious reawakening of his soul, but instead, it proved a terrible blunder. Heartache's heavy shackles were only made heavier by greed.

Twenty-two chests were smashed open by the crew. Gold doubloons spilled on the deck by the thousands, and they lifted them gaily overhead, spilling them through their fingers into piles at their feet. They rolled into the corners of the deck with the rocking of the ocean. In the celebration that followed, the men agreed that if they returned home, the treasure would be claimed by the Grimsby Deep Sea Fishing Company. With England no longer an option, the decision was made to sail to the mainland and live as rich men in Africa where they could each have a palace and a harem of their own. While concocting their plan to vanish into the French colony of Gabon and then farther into the wild continent, Braddock slipped below deck and retrieved his clothing. He dressed and warmed as they murmured above deck about disposing of him. Acting fast, he put the meager possessions he owned into his satchel and collected some items lying about that may benefit his escape. When the moment was right, he escaped through an aft hatch, slipping silently into the water while the crew still celebrated, blinded by their murderous greed.

Braddock swam with every drop of strength that he could muster and managed to reach the shore of Annobón before the horde learned of his escape. He pointed himself down the virgin coast and began to run sluggishly in the scorching hot sand. The sweet smell of salty air mixed with the blossoming flora along the tree line and found its way through his tangled beard. He gazed at the wall of unfamiliar trees and twisted vines that ran along the beach, swallowing the sunlight. Looking over his shoulder at the ship anchored far off the coast, he saw ants spilling over the side into a rowboat, fierce and bloodthirsty.

Braddock's weary legs carried him as far as his strength allowed. He only stopped when he saw a break in the trees. Hastily, he squeezed his body through the small space where sunlight peeked through and spilled onto the shore of a hidden lagoon. Wanting to soak the beauty of the surroundings deep into his temporal lobe, he allowed himself a glance at the serenity of the flawless lagoon which lay before him. A moment which would later prove paramount, as the memory of the lagoon served as a place of refuge while locked away in the dark of his cell.

A short while later, he heard the whoops and taunts of the crew passing the chink in the vines behind him. He sunk into the water and swam out to a small island in the center of the lagoon.

For seven days, he stayed hidden from the world and the madness on this private island. There he slept soundly under the canopy of a sprawling African mahogany tree and listened to the sweet sound of the songbirds gathered in its branches. He ate wild custard apples that sprouted alongside a basin collecting rainwater. He bathed himself in the clear water and washed away the wretched sin that this treasure had sprung upon him. On the eighth day, he ventured back out to the beach and found the ship had raised anchor and disappeared somewhere over the horizon. He was marooned.

Braddock walked down the beach until he came upon a lively fishing hamlet. Moving past a small dock and taking stock of the archaic fleet, he soon came upon the villagers and what remained of their little paradise. They shuttled bags of ocean water from the shoreline and used the liquid to douse the few scattered fires still burning in the aftermath of the passing horde. He had a vision of a bucket brigade he was once part of as a boy. The smell of char and flesh filled his nostrils. Braddock quickly learned that the dark-skinned inhabitants were masters of spearfishing when the instrument of their trade grazed his face, impaling a nearby tree.

"Monstros! Monstros!"

He knew the monsters they spoke of. As they passed by searching for him, they razed the village and relieved their aggression on the locals. Faced with another group of people that wanted him dead, Braddock had a choice to make. Run from the village into the uncharted jungle or head towards the beach and commandeer one of the small boats he saw while observing the town. So, with some wild apples and a basket of fish left behind in the boat, Braddock was once again underway. As he commanded his skeleton to head east toward the coast of Africa, he sat and watched the vivid sunset off the stern. Groping around inside his leather satchel, he removed a small cloth pouch and reached his hand into it. He smiled a survivor's smile as he floated weightlessly on the sea and watched the amber sunset reflect off the water and illuminate the gold doubloons in his hand.

~

"Mr. Braddock? Where is the gold? The gold that will provide some evidence to your defense?"

"It is gone. My satchel was lost in the storm that washed me ashore in France." His gaze scraped the dirt floor.

"Why didn't you make landfall before then?"

"I wanted to go home. I knew if I followed the coast that I would eventually reach Europe and France, and maybe Brittany, where I hoped you had gone to that night so long ago."

Georges sat idle, unable to find the words to explain to his friend the punishment he faced. In those moments in the darkness, Georges found it painful to speak, but he thought it necessary for Braddock to hear it from a familiar voice.

"Mr. Braddock, I fear the authorities do not believe your story. I would try to help you, but the tribunal established to decide your fate will not take the word of someone like me. The families of the dead," he paused, "supposedly dead crew are calling for your head. A part of me understands their skepticism. After all, it is a fantastical tale."

"Is that to say you don't believe me?"

Georges tapped his fingers nervously for a moment, searching his heart.

"Unfortunately, it does not matter if I believe you or not. Your fate is now in the hands of the tribunal.

I fear that without evidence of your story, you appear to be guilty or just plain mad. That seems to be enough for them. They are calling you the Coward of Grimsby. They say you conned the crew and then abandoned them to the depths of the ocean. You should never have returned. You would have been better off making port somewhere along the coast, like Casablanca, and living out your days with another name, importing Honeybush tea."

They sat in their cells in silence. They both knew this would be the last time they would speak, but for Braddock, it was truly bittersweet. This was the last time he would ever talk with someone who believed his account of the doomed voyage. Georges lifted himself off the ground and wiped his dirty palms on his trousers, placed his hat back on his head, and leaned in close to the wall.

"Although I am not stuck behind these walls, Mr. Braddock, I am burdened with the knowledge that my childish dreams and family legends began this tragic turn of events. For that, my friend, I am sorry."

Georges called for the guard to release him from the cell and didn't stop walking until he was at the water's edge. He knew that his stay on the shores of England had run its course, and, with the few shillings left to his name, he purchased passage back across the channel to his homeland. While watching the majesty of the Dover cliffs fade away into the early morning fog, Georges took a pull from his tobacco pipe and clutched his jacket tighter against the cold. He closed his eyes to the wind and cursed adventure, King Ferdinand, Napoleon, and the high seas.

The Grimsby Deep Sea Fishing Company needed to save face and provide the workers of its fleet, its shareholders, and the public with an unwavering message: trifling with them or their property would be dealt with swiftly and harshly. From the moment Braddock's reappearance made headlines until the company was eventually bought out years later, not a single vessel was misappropriated, stolen, or ill-treated. The consensus was that this was a direct result of the punishment doled out to Cornelius Braddock.

Even while on the gallows, he professed his innocence. His assertion that the men were still alive and had abandoned their families for riches sat poorly with the widows. They carried out his sentence swiftly to silence his lies and allow closure to overshadow their grief. Before Braddock was hanged, the Magistrate appointed to oversee the case spoke. His remarks were legal in nature, but the onlookers were held in rapture, waiting to extract their pound of flesh. He added personal comments on the professionalism and nautical excellence of Captain Solomon Gibson and his crew. He spoke of the remorse felt by all that they were defrauded with promises of lifelong riches that they would undoubtedly share with their family and community. The crowd cheered as he gave his closing statement.

"...and on the charges of barratry, theft, and subsequent desertion resulting in the deaths of eight crew members and complete loss of a salvage vessel, Cornelius Braddock is found to be guilty on all counts and shall be hanged from the neck until he is dead. This sentence is to be carried out immediately."

Unable to see the crowd from underneath the dark hood and just before the wooden floor disappeared beneath his feet, Braddock thought of his beloved wife, Rebecca. He wondered if she would meet him someplace after death. He wondered if he would be able to smell her orange blossom perfume and feel the silk fabric of her nightdress against his skin. He hoped she had learned to recreate his mother's familiar recipes, including the *Breton galette saucisse*, which he ate by the cartload as a child.

Most of all, he hoped that wherever he saw her again, it was in a place where he couldn't see the ocean.

SOME YEARS LATER, after life in Grimsby returned to normal and the body of Cornelius Braddock was long interred in a potter's field, a young man strolled along the ramparts of Saint-Malo. Having just entered his adolescent years, Pierre Fournier brandished the beginnings of a wispy mustache and a stray patch of whiskers on his chin. His gangly frame moved playfully atop the stone fortifications while enjoying a brief respite from work. He chewed on a chunk of baguette smothered in creamy, rich butter and fought with the seagulls angling for the crumbs.

After finishing his bread and declaring victory in his battle with the gulls, Pierre made his way back into the stonework maze of streets. He headed towards the bakery, where he worked each day after finishing his studies. Like most teenagers, he was distracted easily. Rather than working, he wished to search for specimens for his collection. He wanted to laugh and dig his feet into the sand with his classmates. Items he found washed up on the beach over the years invaded his bedroom. The small boxes were cataloged and categorized like an archeologist would do. His mother eventually gave up trying to curb his enthusiasm for bringing home such things and began allowing him to trail sand through her kitchen while she baked.

He had stones and bits of rope, mollusk shells, and colorful bits of buoy from the fishermen's pots. Random debris and curiosities that wash up in storms. Sometimes he found luggage that fell from steamships as they passed by on their way to England. He even found an anchor made of iron which his mother helped haul home from the shore. If he closed his window in the summer months, a briny smell would waft through the house, forcing Murielle outside to catch her breath.

As Pierre entered the bakery, the front door struck a shiny bronze bell hanging over it, and a chime sounded. He walked past the glass display cases with the establishment's name painted elegantly on them in delicate black letters, *Le Chocolat de Murielle*. Pierre hung his tattered satchel on a hook behind the bakery's door and greeted his mother with a kiss. A tiny bit of flour transferred to his whiskers from her cheek, and she wiped it away with fingers moistened lovingly with her tongue.

"Such a handsome boy," Murielle Fournier said.

"Mother, please!" Pierre looked around the bakery to find witnesses to this gushing display of love. Luckily for him, the bakery was empty except for one elderly gentleman sitting quietly in the corner, sipping tea. After regaining his masculine composure, Pierre went about his work as his mother disappeared into the storeroom.

"Your mother is lovely," the older man said to

him as Pierre picked up his empty plate. Statements like this no longer surprised Pierre. His mother was considered by many to be the most beautiful woman in Saint-Malo. Since she opened the bakery just a few years prior and bestowed her delicious confections upon the masses, he witnessed his fair share of ogling and long, unnecessary lunch breaks.

"Yes, sir," Pierre replied respectfully and continued his duties, cleaning fingerprints from the glass covering the macaron display.

"People speak of her pain au chocolat all over the province, and I have finally made the trip to taste it for myself. Which, as you see, is difficult for me." He motioned to a single leg underneath the table.

"Yes, sir, it has always been my favorite."

"Your name is Pierre, is it not?" the man asked.

"Yes, sir." His head perked up.

"It is not *Peere*?"

"It is Pierre, sir, after my father."

The man nodded his head slowly and smiled.

"That would make sense. Pierre. My father's brother was named Pierre. It is a common enough name. But what one does with their name is what matters in the end, I suppose. I hope that some will speak my name with a reverence once I pass on. Do you wish the same?" he asked the boy.

"I suppose I do, sir," Pierre answered with little thought.

"My name is Georges Dufort. Perhaps you will remember it with fondness after I make my journey beyond the veil," he said casually.

"I will, sir," Pierre acquiesced.

A few moments passed while Pierre worked, feeling the eyes of Georges upon him.

"How long has your mother owned this fine bakery?" Georges said.

"She purchased it not long ago from Madame Cuvier. She was too old to bake, and her pastries were never delicious."

"It is impressive. It must have been costly," Georges said.

Pierre quickly shuffled his feet, not knowing which direction to turn to escape the conversation.

"I realize the statement is uncivil, but in my old age, I find that people allow me a bit of incivility."

"A relative of mine, ours, died suddenly, passed away, I mean, and left an inheritance to my mother."

Georges took a long, slow sip of tea, slurping the last dregs through his mustache.

"Well, that is very fortunate. I wonder how I would have invested such an inheritance."

The room grew quiet again, and Pierre was at a loss. He looked around quickly for his mother.

She then appeared from the small back storeroom and strode across the floor, leaving her signature trail of flour and perfume in the air. She untied her apron and hung it on the hook near the front door. In the same motion, she retrieved the canvas satchel belonging to her son from the adjacent hook and slung it over her shoulder. She turned to face Pierre and Georges.

"Pierre, please see that Mr. Dufort has your attention while I make a trip to the grocer. Ratatouille for dinner?"

Pierre nodded his approval.

She smiled pleasantly at Georges and kissed her son again on the cheek before leaving. As the canvas satchel swung slightly closer to Georges' view, he caught a glimpse of the faded letters embroidered on the front of it, weathered and baked pale by the sun.

"C. Braddock"

Murielle strolled away down the skinny cobblestone street, half her face hidden in the shadow cast by the medieval facades and half her face made radiant by the sun, beaming with joy. Pierre, now alone with Georges, continued to shine the glass display case. Taking great care not to look directly at the older man, he finally made his way across the floor, but Georges stood quickly.

"Well, Pierre, I must leave now. I thank you for your exquisite service and enlightening conversation." Georges affixed an old captain's hat atop his head and buttoned his deep blue pea coat.

"Thank you, sir. I hope the rest of the day treats you well," Pierre said.

Georges made his way to the door and opened it slightly, just enough to ring the bell, and came to an abrupt stop. He released the door handle and it closed, ringing the bell again in short succession with the last chime. He turned toward the boy.

"I once had a dear friend who told me a great and improbable tale—a tale I wish with all my heart to believe. I yearn to speak his name and remember it with fondness. I believe inside the walls of this lovely bakery is the only place he is remembered fondly. His name was...."

Georges parted his lips to speak the name, but emotion overtook him. The last years were dreadfully painful for him, and a final chance to discover the truth about the ordeal and the treasure was now in the hands of the young man standing before him.

Pierre moved closer to him and whispered.

"Cornelius Braddock."

Georges looked at the young man through wide, tearful eyes. Underneath his civilized but full beard, the beginnings of a smile took shape.

"And the gold?"

Pierre quickly disappeared into the back room and returned a moment later. A youthful grin stretched from ear to ear as he gently placed a small piece of baker's parchment in Georges' open palm. On the parchment was a single pastry. The same pain au chocolat that once satisfied the cravings of Napoleon Bonaparte and nourished the wounded soul of Cornelius Braddock back to health. It was warm and flaky, sprinkled lightly with flecks of sea salt. Georges felt the fresh heat seep into his skin and the strong chocolate aroma awakened the part of his brain where he stored childhood fantasies and memories of the sea. Slowly raising the delicacy to his mouth, he took a bite. His eyes closed as he savored the warmth and sweetness of the confection and the abundance of treasure within.

ABOUT THE AUTHOR

Eric Daniel Ryan is an award-winning author who lives with his family just north of Boston in the shadows of Old Salem Village, the Rebecca Nurse Homestead, and Lovecraft's Arkham Asylum. After studying screenwriting and film production at the School of Visual Arts, he served three years in the US Army and is a combat veteran of the war in Iraq. In 2005 Eric became a Boston Firefighter and, in 2017, opened a business selling and collecting rare, original movie posters called, Vintage Film Art. Each night, after tucking the little ones into bed, he settles down in his two-hundred-year-old home to finish his first novel.

He is the recipient of the 2022 eLit Book Awards Gold Medal for Short Story Fiction and Silver Medal for Historical Fiction. He was a Finalist for the 2022 Next Generation Indie Book Awards - Novella and a Silver Medal Winner in the Short Story/Novella category at the 2022 Readers' Favorites International Book Awards.

www.ingramcontent.com/pod-product-compliance
Lightning Source LLC
Chambersburg PA
CBHW021751190726
48290CB00008B/2572